WHO'S ILL TOL....

WHO'S ILL TODAY?

by Lynne Cherry

BEAVER BOOKS

A Beaver Book
Published by Arrow Books Limited
62-5 Chandos Place, London WC2N 4NW
An imprint of Century Hutchinson Ltd
London Melbourne Sydney Auckland
Johannesburg and agencies throughout the world
First published in Great Britain in 1988 by Andersen Press Ltd
Beaver edition 1989
Published in the United States by E. P. Dutton, New York
Copyright © Lynne Cherry 1988
Printed and bound in Italy by Grafiche AZ, Verona
ISBN 0 09 960750 6

This book is dedicated to
Nancy and David Dougherty, Nancy Drye and Bob Thomas,
Gloria and Walt Hallagan, Ellen Calmus, Jim Huffman
and the house on Rosedale Road.

Who's ill today?

Beavers with fevers,

a snake with an ache,

a small red fox with chicken pox.

Who's at the doctor today?

A whale on a scale,

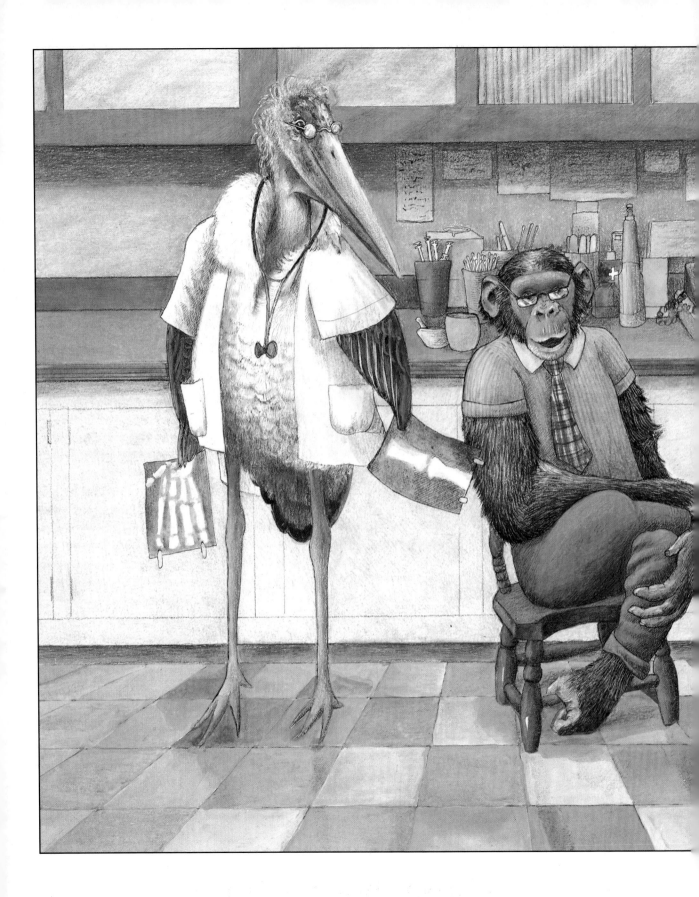

a chimp with a limp,

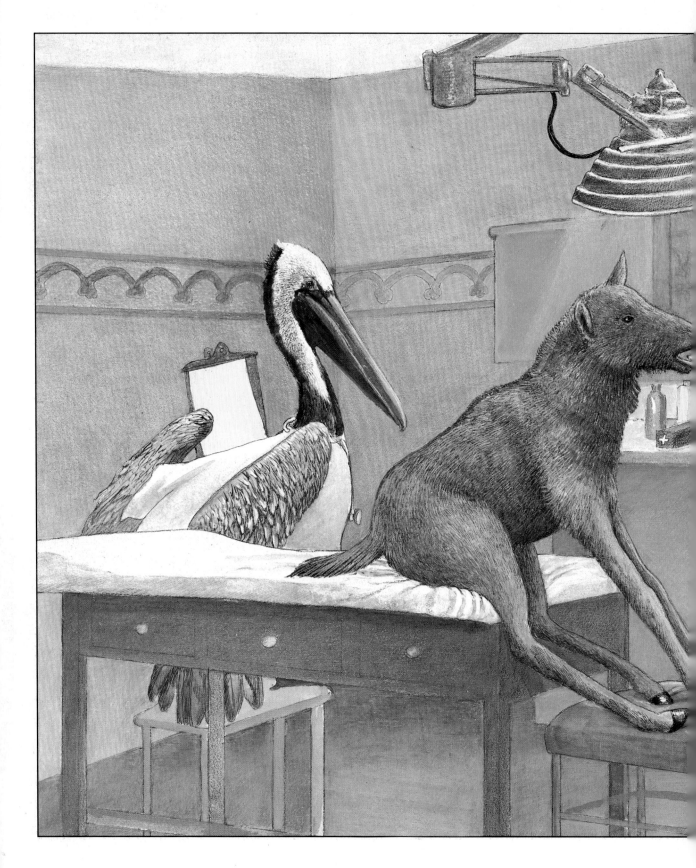

a gnu with the flu.

Who's in the hospital today?

Llamas in pyjamas,

young stoats with sore throats,

cranes with pains,

possums with blossoms,

and baboons with balloons.

Who's all better today?
A porcupine who's feeling fine!

Other titles in the Beaver/Sparrow Picture Book series: